THE PUPPY PLACE

TEDDY

THE PUPPY PLACE

Don't miss any of these other stories by Ellen Miles!

Bandit	Moose
Baxter	Muttley
Bear	Noodle
Bella	Patches
Buddy	Princess
Chewy and Chica	Pugsley
Cocoa	Rascal
Cody	Rocky
Flash	Scout
Goldie	Shadow
Honey	Snowball
Jack	Sweetie
Lucky	Teddy
Lucy	Ziggy
Maggie and Max	

THE PUPPY PLACE

TEDDY

ELLEN MILES

SCHOLASTIC INC.

For Teddy

ISBN 978-0-545-46239-6

Cover art by Tim O'Brien
Original cover design by Steve Scott

12 11 10 9 8 7 6 5 4 3 2   12 13 14 15 16 17/0

Printed in the U.S.A.   40

First printing, October 2012

CHAPTER ONE

Lizzie Peterson flopped down on her bed. "Aaaah," she sighed. She was tired, but happy. Triple A Dynamic Dog Walkers had really taken off lately. She and her best friend, Maria, were business partners. They had started small but now they walked up to twelve dogs a day, every day, after school. This Tuesday afternoon had been a busy one, but Lizzie knew that every dog on their route had gotten plenty of attention and exercise, not to mention pats and love. She felt good about that.

Afterward, Lizzie had come right home and whipped through all her homework. Now there was still a half hour left before dinnertime, and it was Charles's turn to set the table. Lizzie smiled to herself as she picked up the brand-new iPod she'd bought with her hard-earned dog-walking money. As long as they helped with chores, maybe little brothers were worth all the bother. And soon, she thought with a smile, the Bean (her youngest brother, whose real name was Adam) would be old enough to help, too. Then she'd have even more free time.

Lizzie popped in her earbuds and plugged in the cord. She leaned back onto her comfy pillows and scrolled through her song list to find the one she wanted to hear. Wanted? More like *needed*. Lately Lizzie was in love with a song called "Angel Mine" by Toni Bleu. There was just something about it, the way the singer's voice wove the melody around the beat of the drums and the strum of the guitar. The song gave Lizzie tingles every time she heard it. She loved to sing along, even though Charles made fun of the way she sounded when she had her earbuds in. The words were kind of sappy, but Lizzie didn't care.

Angel Mine, you're the dear one,
Angel Mine, be with me now.
Angel Mine, I'll always love you,
Angel Mine, that is my vow.

Lizzie knew that the song was meant to be a guy singing to a girl he loved, but in secret she liked to imagine herself singing it to a dog. Someday, when Lizzie was grown, she knew she would have a dog that was hers alone, her very own dog that she didn't have to share with anyone. She loved Buddy, her family's adorable brown-and-white puppy, and she often sang silly songs to him. But Buddy belonged to all the Petersons. He slept in Charles's room most nights, hung out in their mom's office while she worked on her newspaper articles during the day, and happily greeted each family member whenever they came home. They all loved Buddy, and Buddy loved them back. Lizzie knew she was lucky to have a puppy in the family. But still, she longed for a dog of her very own.

"*Angel Mine*," she sang, as her eyes slid over the "Dog Breeds of the World" poster that hung near her bed. If she could have any dog, which breed would she choose?

Maybe she'd pick a fluffy white Samoyed, or a huge tawny mastiff. She considered the saluki, an elegant Egyptian breed, or a ropy-haired Bergamasco, from Italy. It was hard to choose. She got up and went over to look at her collection of glass dog figurines, picking each one up for the thousandth time. She liked to arrange them in different groupings, according to whether the dogs would get along and be friends. She knew the characteristics of every breed: labs were friendly and athletic, bulldogs were clownish and stubborn, poodles were energetic and smart. And every individual dog within a breed had a personality, too. She believed her glass poodle loved to go for rides in the car, and the bulldog was a snuggle bug. The golden retriever had a favorite toy it carried around, and the Great Pyrenees was a very picky eater. Every dog was different.

That was one reason Lizzie loved fostering puppies. For some time now, her family had been taking in puppies who needed homes, caring for each one until they could find it the perfect owner. Lizzie and her family had gotten to know all kinds of puppies: big puppies, small puppies, fluffy puppies, and smart puppies. They'd cared for lazy puppies and brave puppies, spoiled puppies and wild ones. Lizzie had loved every single one of them. It was never easy to give them up when the time came, but it was always a great feeling to see a puppy find a happy forever home.

Lizzie sighed and flopped back down on her bed. Even though she didn't have a dog of her very own yet, she was so lucky. Her life was full of dogs. She had Buddy. She had her foster pups. She had the dogs she and Maria walked every day. Then there were the dogs at her aunt Amanda's doggy day care, where Lizzie helped out sometimes, and the dogs at Caring Paws Animal Shelter, where Lizzie volunteered on Saturdays. All dogs, all the time. Could life get any better?

Lizzie settled into her pillows and pushed the "play" button again to listen to her favorite song for the fifth time in a row. *"Angel Mine,"* she sang along drowsily, *"you're the dear one."*

Suddenly, she popped up, eyes wide open. Someone was knocking on her door. "Lizzie?" Mom called, as she pushed open the door. "Are you sleeping?"

Lizzie rubbed her eyes. Had she been sleeping? Maybe she had dozed off for a moment. "I'm awake," she said.

Mom came over to touch her forehead. "You're not sick, are you?" she asked.

Lizzie yawned and shook her head. "I'm fine."

Mom frowned. "You've been working hard lately with all these dogs," she said. "Maybe you and Maria need to think carefully about taking on so many clients. And maybe you could think about something other than dogs once in a while. You need some balance in your life. I don't want you to get sick, and I don't want your schoolwork to suffer. . . ."

"I already did my homework." Lizzie didn't need to hear the rest: she'd listened to this lecture before, many times. She pointed to her desk, with her folders all neatly lined up. She knew Mom would never let her keep her business going if her grades started to slip.

Mom nodded. "Okay," she said. "I guess I'm just surprised to find you asleep in the evening. You didn't even hear the phone ring, did you?"

"The phone?" Lizzie asked.

"Dr. Gibson just called," said Mom. "She needs our help with a puppy."

CHAPTER TWO

That woke Lizzie up in a hurry. She sat up and looked around the room for her sneakers. "A puppy? Great! What kind? Are we going to pick him up right now?" She could be ready in about two seconds to head over to the veterinarian's office.

Mom sighed, but she was smiling. "We're not picking up any puppies. Dr. Gibson is coming over to talk to us." She shook her head. "Why this kind of thing always has to happen right at dinner-time, I don't know. . . ."

"But what *breed* is it?" Lizzie asked. Who cared about dinnertime when they had a new puppy coming to stay? Mom always concentrated on the wrong things.

Mom held up her hands. "I don't know anything more than what I've told you. Dr. Gibson sounded upset when she called. She said we were the only people she could think of to help with this puppy."

Lizzie frowned. "The only people? Hmm, that's interesting." Then she brightened. "Well anyway, we have a new puppy to foster."

"Whoa, there, kiddo," said Mom. "Not so fast. I didn't promise to foster any puppy. I just said Dr. Gibson could come by to talk over the issue. That's all. We'll have a Peterson powwow and decide as a family, once we know more." She reached out to hug Lizzie. "Patience, sweetie," she murmured into Lizzie's hair.

Ha. Patience. How could anybody be patient about a puppy? Just then, Lizzie heard the doorbell ring. She dashed out of her room and clattered down the stairs.

When Lizzie threw open the door, there was Dr. Gibson, standing on the front porch with a tiny ball of orange fluff cradled in her arms. "Hello, Lizzie," she said. "Meet Teddy."

Lizzie stared. "That's a *puppy*?" She opened the door wider to let Dr. Gibson walk in. The tiny thing looked more like a stuffed toy. Lizzie took a closer look. Then she grinned. "He's a Pomeranian, isn't he?"

Dr. Gibson nodded. "Exactly right. And I know you like big dogs better, but wait till you get to know this guy. You're going to love him." She handed the puppy to Lizzie while she took off her coat. "He's a bit sleepy at the moment."

Lizzie stared down at the puppy in her arms. He hardly weighed a thing. He blinked up at her with shiny black button eyes and opened his tiny mouth in a yawn, his little pink tongue curling lazily. Teddy had a pointy snout and pricked-up triangular ears, and with that reddish-orange coat he looked almost like a baby fox. His fluffy fur stood in a ruff around his neck and shoulders, and when Lizzie stroked him she saw that his tail, also fluffy, curled over his back.

"Wow," she said. "He's pretty cute. For a small dog, I mean. And I can see where he got his name — he looks just like a teddy bear."

"He's really smart, too," said Dr. Gibson. "And courageous. He thinks he's a big boy. Better keep an eye on him and Buddy when they first meet. I've seen some Pomeranians who think they can take on Great Danes. Teddy's only about a year old, but he's very mature for his age."

By this time, Mom had come downstairs, too. She gasped when she saw the puppy Lizzie held. "But —" She turned to Dr. Gibson. "I didn't realize you were bringing a puppy over right away."

Dr. Gibson looked down at her shoes. "I know. I'm sorry. But this all came up so suddenly. I just didn't have any choice. I can't leave him at the office, and I can't take him with me, either. I'm on my way to visit a friend who has a very old, sick dog. Anyway, I was, uh, really hoping you could help."

Mom softened. "We're always glad to help with puppies," she said. "But why the big emergency? Where did this pup come from?"

Lizzie looked up just in time to see Dr. Gibson gesture silently toward the living room. She watched Mom and the vet slip off to talk privately. She was curious, but right now she had more important things on her mind. She already knew she wanted to foster this puppy, but she had to know if he and Buddy would get along. "Hey,

Mr. Teddy." She stroked the dog's apple-sized head with one finger. "How would you like to meet the rest of the family?"

Dad and the boys were out in the backyard, playing T-ball with Buddy as an extra outfielder. Charles was way beyond T-ball and always said he only played so the Bean could learn to hit, but Lizzie could tell he still loved whacking the ball off the tee with the big yellow plastic bat.

"Look what I have," Lizzie called. In her arms, Teddy stirred and began to struggle to get down. She tightened her grip. First she had to make sure that Buddy would be friendly.

"Whoa, what's that?" Charles came charging over to see. "It looks like a —"

"A fox, right?" Lizzie asked. "I know. It's a Pomeranian."

Dad came over, holding the Bean's hand. "Be

very gentle," he told the Bean. "Remember, little puppies like this can get hurt easily."

The Bean reached up to pet Teddy very carefully with one pudgy finger.

Buddy put his front paws up on Lizzie's leg and sniffed at the fluffy pup. His tail wagged and he gave a happy little bark.

That did it. With a surprisingly strong kick, Teddy leapt out of Lizzie's arms and joined Buddy on the ground, barking joyously and spinning around in circles. He spun so fast that he looked like an orange blur.

Oh, yay! Another dog! Let's play! Let's play! Let's play!

His fluffy tail waved and wagged as he and Buddy raced around.

"I guess they get along," Dad shouted over the barking.

The Bean put his fingers in his ears. "Too loud, too loud," he wailed.

Lizzie had to agree. Like many small dogs, Teddy had a loud, piercing bark. And it just didn't stop. He yipped and yapped and barked, on and on, long after Buddy had stopped barking. Lizzie almost felt like putting her fingers in her ears, too.

"Where's his 'off' switch?" Dad yelled.

"Be quiet, you," yelled Charles.

"Don't yell at him," Lizzie yelled. "It just makes him think you're barking along with him." She remembered reading that somewhere.

Mom came out the back door and stood gaping at the scene.

Lizzie swooped down and picked up the small orange fluff ball. "Shhh, shhh." She held him close. Teddy's barks died down until he was quiet again.

"We're going to have to do something about that," Dad said. "I mean, if we're going to foster this puppy."

Mom looked doubtful. "I'm not sure there's much we *can* do," she said. "That barking is exactly why Teddy is here right now." She pulled Dad aside and spoke to him in a low voice, waving a hand at Teddy.

"What?" Lizzie asked. "What are you telling him? If it's about Teddy, I need to know." She put Teddy down and walked over to tug on Mom's sleeve. Teddy began to bark again, but Lizzie hardly noticed. She looked at Dad. "Dad?" she asked.

Dad's face had turned very solemn. He glanced at Mom, then back at Lizzie. "Come inside," he said.

CHAPTER THREE

Lizzie gathered Teddy up into her arms. He quieted down right away. She followed Mom and Dad inside and they all sat down at the kitchen table. "You're not going to like this," Mom said to Lizzie. "Dr. Gibson —"

"Where is Dr. Gibson, anyway? Did she leave?" Lizzie interrupted.

"She went to visit her friend," Mom said, "the one with the old dog."

Lizzie pictured an older dog with a white muzzle. "Is her friend's dog dying?" she asked. "Is that what you didn't want to tell me?"

Mom looked at Dad. "No," she said. "That wasn't it. It's about Teddy, and why his owners gave him up."

"There's an operation," Dad said. "It's called debarking. The dog's vocal cords are cut so that when he tries to bark, he hardly makes any sound. Teddy's owners brought him to Dr. Gibson hoping she would do it."

"What?" Lizzie yelled. "Why would anybody *do* that to a dog?" Startled, Teddy jumped out of her arms and began to spin around on the slippery kitchen floor. His yipping and yapping filled the room. Lizzie picked him up again, shushing him as she paced around the kitchen. "That's terrible! How can they do that? Dogs need to bark so they can communicate with other dogs and with people. How would Teddy's owners like it if someone cut *their* vocal cords and they couldn't talk?" She buried her nose in Teddy's fluffy ruff. She felt like crying. How could people be so mean to animals?

"A lot of people feel that way," Mom said. "In fact, Dr. Gibson said that debarking is illegal in some countries and in some states in this country. But it's not against the law in our state."

Lizzie sat down again and squeezed Teddy even tighter. "I won't let them do it. I won't. I'll run away with him and hide him so nobody can ever find him. We'll go to a place where it's illegal. We'll —"

"Hold on there." Dad put a hand on her arm. "You don't have to run away. Nobody's going to debark this dog. At least, Dr. Gibson isn't going to."

"That's right," Mom said. "She refused to do the operation. Not only that, she told the people that she did not think they were the right owners for

Teddy, and offered to find him another home. She didn't want them taking him to another vet who might do the operation. Surprisingly, they agreed."

"What's so surprising about it?" Lizzie asked. "Obviously, they didn't love him. Otherwise, why would they even consider —"

The back door slammed, and Charles and the Bean charged into the kitchen with Buddy at their heels.

Teddy leapt off Lizzie's lap and began to spin in circles again, barking at the top of his little lungs.

Look! New people just came in. Look, everybody! Look!

Dad put his fingers in his ears. "I think I can kind of understand how somebody might —"

Mom gave him a sharp look and he stopped. But she didn't look happy about the noise Teddy was making, either. Quickly, Lizzie scooped the little dog into her arms. Teddy's barks got a little quieter, but this time he did not stop completely. "We can foster him, right?" she asked over the noise.

"Do you really want to?" her dad asked. "I mean, really? You don't even like little dogs."

Lizzie nodded firmly. "I like this one," she said. And she did. There was something about Teddy, despite all the barking. With that big personality and adorable foxy face, he was easy to love. "Somebody has to help this dog. Otherwise he'll never find a loving home."

Charles frowned. "What if he never stops barking?" he asked.

"*Arf! Arf, arf, arf!*" barked the Bean. "I can bark all the time, too."

Mom rolled her eyes. "One yippy yapper is enough." She picked the Bean up for a hug. Then she gave Lizzie a serious look. "This might not be easy," she said. "It'll be a lot of work to teach him to be quieter, won't it?"

"I helped Cody," Lizzie reminded her. "And Chica, remember?" Both foster puppies had been barkers. Cody was an excitable Dalmatian puppy who had matured a lot in the time the Petersons had cared for him. And Chica the Chihuahua had improved, too.

"That's true," said Dad. "You worked hard with both of those puppies."

By now, Teddy had quieted down in Lizzie's arms. But he was alert and watchful; his bright button eyes moved from person to person as they spoke. "Dr. Gibson said he was smart," Lizzie said. "All I'm asking for is the chance to try."

Mom looked at Dad. Dad looked at Mom.

"Let's give it a week," said Mom. "I think that's about all I can take if he doesn't learn. And you have to promise to keep up with your homework, too."

Dad nodded. "Sounds good to me. Charles? What do you and the Bean think?"

They were both standing by Lizzie's chair, petting Teddy's fluffy fur. "Okay with me," Charles said, "as long as he's Lizzie's responsibility."

"Me, too!" The Bean giggled as Teddy licked his fingers.

"I hereby declare this Peterson powwow adjourned," said Dad. "We've made a good family decision — and besides, I'm starving, and I think I smell pot roast."

Mom laughed. "You sure do. Let's get the table set and sit down to dinner."

Lizzie hugged Teddy and whispered into his ear. "You're safe now," she said. He nuzzled her cheek with his nose as if to say "thank you," and Lizzie felt her heart swell. She was sure she could help this noisy pup settle down.

CHAPTER FOUR

As soon as dinner was over, Lizzie took Teddy and Buddy out back for a pee. Then she scooped up the tiny orange pup and headed upstairs. After a quick phone call to Maria to tell her about the newest foster pup, Lizzie brought Teddy into her room. "We're going to figure this out," she told Teddy as she put him down on her bed, "no matter how long it takes."

She began to pull books off her shelf, reading the titles out loud. *"Puppies for Idiots,"* she said. *"Training Your Dog the Positive Way. A Hundred and One Dog Tricks."* She stacked the books on the foot of her bed. Then she pulled out a few more for good measure. "*All About Dogs. Help! My Puppy Is Driving Me Crazy.*" She laughed at the last one. "That's a good one for you, Teddy. You're not driving *me* crazy, but I noticed that Dad's eyes were practically spinning around in his head during your latest bark-a-thon."

She settled herself comfortably on her bed with Teddy on her lap. He was so tiny and weighed so little — even less than some cats Lizzie had held. Maybe even less than Samson, the new class guinea pig at school — who, admittedly, was pretty big for a guinea pig. "Are you sure you're really a dog?" she asked him, using one finger to scratch him between the ears. All dogs liked that. Sure enough, Teddy liked it, too. His eyes blinked closed and he sighed happily, then licked Lizzie's hand. "Well, I guess you are." Lizzie smiled down at him and shrugged. Teddy sighed again and settled in for a nap.

Lizzie opened one of the books in her pile, *All About Dogs*. It was a book about dog breeds, with pictures and lots of information — lots more than fit on her "Dog Breeds of the World" poster. She checked the index in the back for "Pomeranian," then flipped to page 273: "'A member of the Toy group, this spunky breed makes a wonderful companion or assistance dog,'" she read out loud, stroking Teddy's soft fur. "'Brave and confident, smart and trainable. Loves to please.'"

Lizzie grinned. Dr. Gibson was right: she was not usually crazy about smaller dogs. But these personality-filled Pomeranians were like big dogs in tiny dogs' bodies. Reading on, she discovered that Pomeranians were actually descended from big dogs like Samoyeds and huskies, dogs that pulled sleds in the frozen north or herded sheep in the high mountains. "No wonder I like you," she said to Teddy. "Your great-great-great-great-great-great-grandparents *were* big dogs."

She read that Pomeranians were playful, enthusiastic, and energetic. Since they were also very sensitive and tuned in to their owners' wishes, they were often used as therapy dogs. "How about that, Teddy?" she asked. Teddy snorted a tiny little snore and squiggled down in her lap, making himself more comfortable. Lizzie laughed and petted him. All this breed talk must be making him sleepy.

Lizzie put that book aside and started to leaf through the other ones, looking for advice on how to stop a dog from barking. There was a lot of information. "I'll never remember all this," she said to herself. She picked the little pup up off her lap and got up to find a notebook, a pen, and some sticky notes. Then she settled in again, with

Teddy curled up next to her on a pillow. Asleep, he looked exactly like a stuffed toy.

"Maybe that's what your first owners really wanted," Lizzie murmured, touching his soft ears. "A pretend dog. They couldn't deal with a real-dog who did real dog things like barking."

Poor Teddy. It wasn't his fault. It said right in the breed information that Pomeranians were known for barking a lot. His owners should have checked that out before they decided what kind of dog to get.

Lizzie began to read and take notes. She had learned a little about barking problems when they had fostered Cody, but this time she learned a lot more.

She learned that dogs bark for all kinds of reasons: boredom, anxiety about being alone or other worries, excitement (that was Teddy!), fear, and to alert their owners to danger. Or to what they *thought* was danger, like a delivery man coming to the front door. Some dogs barked at other dogs, or *with* other dogs, like if another dog in the neighborhood was barking. And some dogs barked just to get attention.

Lizzie read that it was best to ignore a barking dog, wait until he stopped, then reward him with a treat. She thought about that. Instead of ignoring Teddy's barking, she had scooped him up into her arms. He had quieted down the first few times, but not the last time.

"Oops," she said. Maybe giving him that kind of attention had not been the best way to stop his barking. But how could she ignore that high-pitched yapping that went on and on and on? With Teddy, she might never get to the giving-him-a-treat part.

She read some more. A couple of books suggested that you should spray a barking dog with water, or tap him on the nose, or get a special collar that would shock him, or spritz him with a bad-smelling spray when he barked — but there was no way Lizzie was doing any of those things. She did not like to punish dogs; she liked to train them with praise and treats instead. She tossed those books onto the floor.

One book suggested that you should "interrupt" the barking with a whistle or a clap, then as soon as the dog was quiet for even a second you should praise him and give him a treat. If you added a word when you gave him the treat, like "quiet" or "hush," you could start teaching the dog to quiet down when you said that word.

Lizzie remembered how she and Maria had trained Cody, whose main problem had been barking when someone came to the door. They had set up a situation where Maria came to the door and knocked. Cody started to bark, but

Lizzie waited until he stopped, just to take a breath, then immediately said, "Quiet! Good boy," and gave him a treat. After about a million repetitions, Cody got to the point where he could stay quiet for at least a few seconds before he began barking again. Maybe something like that would work with Teddy.

Lizzie closed the last book and put it on the pile. This wasn't going to be easy, but she was determined to do her best. One thing that all the books agreed on was that it was important to make sure that a barking dog got lots and lots of exercise, since a tired dog was less likely to bark. "That's simple," Lizzie said, looking down at the sleeping puppy on her pillow. "Starting tomorrow, Mr. Teddy Bear, you will be the official mascot of Triple A Dynamic Dog Walkers."

CHAPTER FIVE

"Thirteen dogs?" Maria stared at Lizzie. They were outside at recess time, the first chance Lizzie had found to tell Maria all about her plans for bringing Teddy along when they walked their clients' dogs that afternoon. They sat next to each other on a pair of swings, swaying gently and talking while they watched some other fourth graders play a noisy game of four-square.

"Sure, why not?" Lizzie answered. "If we can handle twelve, we can handle thirteen."

"Well, first of all," said Maria, "we're barely handling twelve. It takes us hours every day, even when we walk the dogs two at a time. And if you have Teddy along you can probably only handle one other dog, so it'll take even longer. But that's not even the point. The point is, thirteen dogs?" She bugged out her eyes. "Thirteen?"

"What?" Lizzie still didn't get it.

"Duh! Thirteen is an unlucky number!" Maria yelled. "Everybody knows that. Walking thirteen dogs is just asking for trouble."

Lizzie burst out laughing. "Oh, come on," she said. "Don't be so superstitious. There's nothing lucky or unlucky about thirteen. It's just a stupid old number."

Maria frowned. "I'm not the only one who's superstitious," she said. "Remember yesterday, you saw a heads-up penny on the floor in the cafeteria? You said it was good luck and grabbed it to put in your pocket."

"Well . . ." Lizzie tried to think of how to explain why that was different.

"And you always make a wish on the first star you see," Maria added. "And on birthday candles, of course. All of that is superstition." She smiled smugly. "So there."

"Fine," said Lizzie. "But I still want to bring Teddy along when we walk dogs today. He really needs the exercise. It might help him quit barking so much."

"Whatever." Maria shrugged. "But remember, I warned you." She pushed off to swing high up into the sky.

Later, after school, Lizzie raced home to get Teddy. He spun and barked when she came in. Instead of yelling for him to be quiet, or picking him up, she quickly clapped her hands and whistled. When he stopped yipping for just one second to cock his head curiously at her, she said, "Good boy."

It worked, kind of. He started to bark again about a half second later. Lizzie sighed as she opened the fridge door, looking for something really good to use for treats. Teddy barked and spun around behind her while she poked through the meat drawer.

Mom appeared in the kitchen, frowning at the noise. She didn't have to say a word. Lizzie knew exactly what her mother was thinking.

"I'm working on it," Lizzie told her as she put a few slices of turkey into a sandwich bag. "Right now I'm just ignoring him until he stops. Like — right now." Teddy had paused, maybe just to take a breath. "Good boy." Lizzie pinched off a tiny bite of the turkey and held it out for Teddy to take. He gobbled it down, then sat back on his butt, his bright eyes focused on Lizzie. And he began to bark again.

That was great, great, great! How about some more, more, more?

Lizzie shrugged and smiled at her mother. "Guess it's going to take some time," she said. "But Dr. Gibson was right that he's a fast learner. Want to see the trick I already taught him this morning?"

Mom put her hands on her hips. "Sure," she said.

Lizzie explained. "First I checked to see what tricks he already knows." She faced Teddy. "Sit, Teddy," she said.

Teddy sat, his eyes glued to Lizzie's. She loved how smart he seemed. It was like he was just waiting to hear what she wanted him to do next.

"Good boy." She gave him a piece of turkey. "Shake," she said, after he'd gobbled it down. Teddy held out his left paw as Lizzie reached with her right hand.

"Good boy," Lizzie said again.

"Cute. Is that the trick?" Mom asked.

"No, he already knew that. Plus 'lie down,' 'stay,' and 'sit pretty.' His first owners must have taught him a lot, even though they couldn't teach him to stop barking. But watch," said Lizzie. She turned back to Teddy. "Give me five," she told the tiny pup.

This time, instead of lifting his left paw, Teddy held up his right paw just as Lizzie held out her right hand again. She slid her hand under his paw so it looked like he was giving her five. "Yes!" she cried. "Good boy." After she'd slipped Teddy some turkey, she turned to her mom, grinning. "He learned that in about three minutes."

Mom nodded. "Very nice. Well, at least he's not barking while he does tricks." She picked up her coffee mug, ready to go back upstairs to her office.

"That's the whole point," said Lizzie. "Now, if he starts to bark, I can ask him to give me five instead. Hopefully it'll distract him enough to make him quit."

Mom raised her eyebrows. "Hopefully. Just don't forget —"

"My homework. I know," said Lizzie. "I only have a few math problems and a spelling quiz to study for, but I promise I'll do it as soon as I get home." She tugged on Teddy's leash. "C'mon, Mr. Yippy. Let's go find Maria."

CHAPTER SIX

Lizzie spotted her friend before Teddy did. Maria was waiting on their usual corner, with two dogs on leashes. She had already picked up Tank, the German shepherd, and Scruffy, a small Maltese–Yorkshire terrier mix whose owner called him a Morkie.

Lizzie waved at her friend, trying to catch Maria's attention without getting Teddy all excited. Maria waved back. "Hey, is that Teddy?" she called.

Oops. Immediately, Teddy started to bark at the top of his lungs, straining at the leash as he tried to run toward Maria and the two dogs.

Who's there? Who's there? Let's see! Let's see! Let's see!

Lizzie realized she and Maria should have made a plan for introducing the dogs, but it was too late now. Teddy was surprisingly strong for such a tiny dog. He dragged Lizzie toward Maria, barking all the way.

Scruffy was a barker, too. He added three yips for every one of Teddy's yaps. By the time Tank joined in with his loud, high-pitched shepherd bark, the noise was overwhelming. Lizzie knew that both of the bigger dogs were usually friendly, but she was still careful to keep a tight hold on Teddy's leash as they approached. The barking quieted down a bit as the three dogs sniffed one another, tails wagging and ears on alert. Then Teddy began to spin in circles, barking excitedly, his fluffy tail waving high over his back and his mouth wide in a doggy grin.

Hurrah! New friends! Hurrah, hurrah, hurrah!

Lizzie clapped her hands and whistled. Teddy paused to look up at her. "Good boy," she said. She dug into her pocket for a scrap of turkey and slipped it into his mouth before he could start barking again.

"Wow." Maria gazed down at Teddy in wonder. "He sure can bark."

"I know," said Lizzie. "I'm working on it."

"He's cute, though," said Maria. "Really cute. And you know it, don't you, little one?" She made a kissy-face at Teddy. "And if he's also as smart as you say he is, someone will want to give him a good home."

"I hope you're right," said Lizzie. Now that the dogs had gotten to know one another a bit, they had calmed down. Lizzie and Maria began to walk their usual route, up toward the school and then back around past the cemetery.

"Are you sure you can handle another dog along with Teddy?" Maria asked doubtfully as they approached the house where Atlas, a golden retriever, lived.

"Positive." Lizzie hoped she sounded more confident than she felt. In truth, she wasn't sure at all. "Let me hold Tank and Scruffy while you go get him. I'll try to keep Teddy from barking when he sees the new dog." She looped Teddy's leash over her arm and put a hand into her pocket to pull off a piece of turkey so she'd be ready.

The second Maria walked away, Tank shoved his nose into Lizzie's hand, trying to get at the turkey. Lizzie turned away from him, trying to keep it out of his reach. Teddy ran around her in circles, trying to see what was going on. Scruffy pushed his head between her knees, sniffing at the sidewalk where a tiny piece of turkey had dropped. Soon Lizzie was wrapped up in three leashes, so tangled that she couldn't take a step in any direction. Her arms were pinned to her sides. She was trapped.

A moment later Maria came out of the house with Atlas at her side. He was a big dog with a lot of energy, but he had very good manners. If you told him to heel, he would stick to your side like glue.

Usually, that is.

That day was different. As soon as he spotted the tangle of dogs, he lunged forward, dragging Maria along behind him. "Heel, Atlas, heel," she cried. He ignored her and charged toward Lizzie.

Teddy started to bark and spin, but Lizzie was too tangled up in the leashes to even try to clap her hands. Scruffy yipped and yapped and dashed toward Atlas. *Wham!* Lizzie went down hard, banging her knee and her elbow. "Ow," she cried. Tank stood over her, drooling as he stared at the turkey in Lizzie's fist. She opened her hand.

"Go ahead," she said wearily. "Eat it."

Maria shook her head. "It's going to be a long day," she said as she helped Lizzie to her feet and began to untangle the leashes.

Maria was right. Somehow, they managed to get all their clients' dogs walked, but it took a lot longer than usual. Lizzie was exhausted by the time she and her friend parted in front of Maria's house. "Phew! Done." Lizzie tried to find the energy to smile. "At least nothing *really* terrible happened, even though we walked thirteen dogs."

Maria rolled her eyes. "I guess you're right," she said. "Still, I vote that you leave Teddy home tomorrow. I can't go through that again."

Lizzie nodded. She couldn't blame her friend for feeling that way. "I'll just take him out after we're done, I guess. Unless I can convince Charles to do it." She waved to Maria and set off for home.

Teddy trotted along beside her, looking like an innocent ball of orange fluff. She smiled down at him and shook her head. "Troublemaker," she said fondly. He barked happily up at her.

And then he kept barking. And barking. And barking.

Lizzie knew she should do the gimme-five thing with him, or clap her hands, or try to teach him the "quiet" command — but just at that moment Lizzie had the strangest thought. It just popped into her mind. *I'm tired of all of these dogs.* She stopped in the middle of the sidewalk, surprised at herself. She had never, ever had a thought like that before. Not in her whole dog-loving life. But suddenly it was all too much: the walking, the training, the constant attention. Dogs, dogs, dogs. She'd had it. She needed a break. Right that moment, she couldn't stand even one second more of Teddy's yapping.

Lizzie pulled her iPod out of her pocket and plugged in her earbuds. She knew it wasn't right. She knew she should deal with Teddy's barking. But at that moment, all she wanted was to tune him out, just for the few minutes it would take to walk home. Besides, she hadn't heard her song since last night. She found "Angel Mine," cranked up the volume, and began to walk dreamily along, holding Teddy's leash in one hand and the iPod in the other.

"Angel Mine, you're the dear one," Lizzie sang along happily as she stepped off the curb to cross the street. She didn't care one bit that she probably sounded like a bellowing moose. *"Angel Mine, be with me — hey!"*

She frowned at Teddy, who was pawing at her leg frantically. "*What*? What do you *want*?" One of her earbuds fell out as she glared down at the tiny dog. That's when she heard it. The howl of an ambulance siren, growing closer every second.

CHAPTER SEVEN

Lizzie took three giant steps backward and sat down — *thump* — on the curb, pulling Teddy into her lap. Her other earbud fell out and her iPod clattered to the sidewalk. "Whoa," she gasped as the ambulance drew closer, its lights flashing and its siren wailing. In the split second that it passed her, Lizzie caught sight of a familiar face through the windshield: Meg Parker, a firefighter who worked with Lizzie's dad. Meg sat in the passenger seat in her blue EMT suit, staring openmouthed at Lizzie as the ambulance whizzed by.

The siren's wail, loudest as the ambulance passed, began to grow distant as the ambulance sped down the street. Lizzie sat on the curb, her heart banging away in her chest. She tightened her grip on Teddy. "Wow. That was a close call," she said into his furry ear.

For once, Teddy was quiet. Lizzie wondered if he was as stunned as she was. That ambulance had come out of nowhere. And now it was gone, and she could barely hear the siren at all. She did hear something, though — a small, tinny sound, like tiny people singing inside a sardine can. She looked down and saw her iPod lying next to her, earbuds still plugged in. "Angel Mine" was still playing. She picked up the iPod and turned it off.

Suddenly, Lizzie never wanted to hear that song again. She could hardly believe that she'd had the volume up high enough to miss the sound of that siren. "Not smart, Lizzie," she said to herself. She knew she had risked her own safety, and Teddy's, too, by tuning out the world that way.

She took a deep breath and stood up. She'd been lucky, and she knew it. Now all she wanted was to be home. "Let's go, Teddy," she said.

A few minutes later, Lizzie let herself in the back door and walked into the kitchen, hoping to find a snack to munch on while she did her homework. Instead, she found her mom, her dad, and Dr. Gibson.

Dad stared at Lizzie with his arms crossed. Mom sat at the kitchen table shaking her head. Dr. Gibson leaned against the doorframe and frowned.

"Elizabeth Maude Peterson," said her dad.

Lizzie blinked. That was *Mom's* thing, the thing she always said when she was really upset with Lizzie. Dad never called her by her whole name like that. She did not like the look on his face. She bent to unclip Teddy's leash.

"Lizzie," Dad said. "Look at me. What just happened out there?"

"Happened?" Lizzie asked. "Nothing. I mean — I'm fine. Teddy's fine, too. Nothing happened."

"That's not what Meg Parker just called to tell me," Dad said. "Meg said that you just almost got run over by an ambulance —"

"Because you had your earbuds in," Mom interrupted. She held out a hand. "And probably with the volume up way too high. Let's have it."

Lizzie knew what she wanted. She pulled her iPod out of her pocket and handed it over.

"You'll get this back when you've convinced me that you can use it responsibly," Mom said as she tucked it into her pocket.

Next it was Dr. Gibson's turn. "What were you thinking?" she asked. "I came by to see how Teddy is doing, and this is what I hear — that

53

you put him in danger. I asked your family to take care of this puppy because you are the best foster family I know. But now —"

Lizzie bit her lip in an effort to stop the tears that felt hot behind her eyes. "I didn't think —" she began.

"No, you didn't." Her dad's harsh look softened as he came over to kneel by Lizzie. "You didn't think, and that's the problem. We're happy you're safe," he said. "But I don't ever want to hear about you doing something like that again, do you understand?"

"Uh-huh." Lizzie looked down at her feet. She had never felt so miserable. Not only had she upset her parents, she had disappointed Dr. Gibson. "I'm really sorry," she said to the floor. "I knew it wasn't right. I just needed a break from Teddy's barking, just for a few minutes."

She looked up in time to see Dr. Gibson nodding.

"Maybe you're beginning to understand how his first owners felt," she said.

"No!" said Lizzie. "I understand that they were frustrated. But I still think they were wrong to want to take away his voice permanently." She bent down and scooped up Teddy, who had been unusually quiet for these few moments. "I mean, look at him. He's a hero. He's the one who let me know the ambulance was coming. He saved my life!"

It was only at that moment that Lizzie understood what had really happened. She explained it all in a rush of words: When he heard the ambulance coming, Teddy had probably tried to get her attention by barking, and when that didn't work he had tried the very trick she had taught him — giving five. He had pawed at her leg to get her attention. What a smartie. She nuzzled her nose into his neck. "Thank you," she whispered.

Then she looked up at the adults in the room. "I promise that from now on I will give Teddy my full attention."

Dr. Gibson came over and put her hands on Lizzie's shoulders. "I know you didn't mean to do anything wrong." She looked straight into Lizzie's eyes. "But to be honest, I am wondering whether you are the right foster family for this dog. I think it might be best if I try to find someone else to care for Teddy until we find him a forever home."

CHAPTER EIGHT

Lizzie stared at Dr. Gibson. "What?" She couldn't believe her ears. "You're going to take Teddy away? Just because I messed up?"

Dr. Gibson put a hand on Lizzie's shoulder. "It's not a punishment, Lizzie. I just get the sense that Teddy is a little — well, a little too much for all of you. Your plate is pretty full, with all your dog walking and other activities. And I can see how Teddy's barking would be very disruptive to your family's life."

"But . . ." Lizzie felt as if she'd been punched in the stomach. "But he was learning. I just need a little more time. And I'll never, never —"

Mom came over to put her arm around Lizzie. "Honey," she said, "I think Dr. Gibson has made a decision, and we have to live with that."

"You don't care." Lizzie jerked away from her mother's touch. "You hate Teddy and his barking. You'll be happy if she takes him away."

"Lizzie." There was a warning tone in Dad's voice. "That's no way to speak to your mother."

"Well . . ." Dr. Gibson looked uncomfortable. "I'm sure it will take me some time to find another foster home. Why don't you keep Teddy for a few more days? I'll be in touch." She grabbed her jacket and left.

Lizzie picked up Teddy and held him close.

He snuffled at her face and licked her cheek.

What's wrong? What's all the fuss about?

Lizzie rubbed her cheek against his. "Don't you worry," she told him. "You're not going anywhere."

"Lizzie." Mom reached out to hug her.

"I have homework to do." Lizzie pulled away. She felt hot tears behind her eyes, and all she wanted was to be alone with Teddy.

She ran upstairs and flung herself on her bed for a good, long cry. Teddy snuggled up next to her on the bed while she sobbed. After she'd cried for a while, she lay there staring up at her dog poster and her dog figurines.

What a joke. She was supposed to be such a dog expert, but she couldn't even take care of one tiny puppy. She ripped down the poster and swept the figurines into a shoe box. She pulled her dog books off the shelf and stuck everything into her closet so she wouldn't have to look at it. Then she lay down and cried some more. When she felt all cried out, she brought Teddy with her down the hall to Mom's study. She had to call Maria. Only a best friend could really understand what she was going through.

"What?" Maria asked, when Lizzie spilled out the story. "Dr. Gibson's going to take him away? Why?"

"Because she doesn't trust me, that's why," Lizzie said. "And maybe she shouldn't. I thought I knew everything about dogs, and that I was the best dog trainer ever. I thought nobody could take care of a puppy as well as I could. I thought —" She began to cry all over again. Teddy put a paw on her arm and looked up at her, blinking with his big round eyes. "I thought all that, but I was wrong. I messed up."

Maria was silent for a moment. "Well, maybe you did. But you really do know a lot about dogs. You just made a mistake. My dad says the important thing is to learn from your mistakes."

Maria was such a good friend. She could have mentioned the whole "thirteen dogs–bad luck" thing. Not Maria. Still, her kind words couldn't take the sting out of what had happened. "I learned, all right," Lizzie said. "I learned that I'm a failure. I can't teach Teddy not to bark. I can't even take care of him right."

"But he took care of you," Maria said. "That was amazing, the way he let you know that the ambulance was coming."

Lizzie sniffed. "I know. He really is smart." She looked down at Teddy on her lap and stroked his soft, fluffy ruff. She felt terrible. She had wanted to help Teddy find the best home, but instead she had put him in danger.

She pictured the scene again. It was like a movie that would play forever in her mind: a horror movie. There she was, about to cross the street with Teddy — right into the path of a speeding ambulance. "I still can't believe I couldn't even hear that siren. I might as well have been completely deaf."

"Lizzie," said Maria after a moment. "That's it!"

"What?" Lizzie asked. "What's it?"

"Teddy could be a hearing-assistance dog. You know, like he could help a deaf person, the same way Simba helps my mom." Maria's mother was blind, but she could go anywhere and do anything because she had an amazing guide dog. "Remember how my pen pal told me her cousin had a hearing dog?" she went on, all in a rush. "Don't you think Teddy would be perfect for that job?"

Lizzie looked down at Teddy, curled up in her lap. "Maybe," she said. "What exactly do they do?"

"I don't know a lot," Maria admitted. "I just know they help alert a deaf person when certain things happen, like when the phone rings. Just the way Teddy alerted you about the siren."

Lizzie felt a growing excitement. "Yeah," she said. "Maybe he *would* be perfect for that." She put Teddy down on the floor and stood up, pacing around the room. "I'll have to do some research, learn more about what they do. Then I'll have to start training him some more. I have a few days to work with him before Dr. Gibson takes him back. If I can just show her —" she stopped. "Maria, do you think you could get someone to help you walk dogs for a couple days? I'll need every minute to work with Teddy."

"Well, I —" Maria began.

"Great," said Lizzie. "Thanks. I have to go. Bye." She hung up, sat down, and spun the chair around to face the computer. It was time to get to work.

CHAPTER NINE

On Sunday night, Lizzie called Dr. Gibson. After four days of working with Teddy, she was too excited to wait any longer. She had to show off what he could do. If this didn't convince Dr. Gibson that Lizzie was a good dog trainer, nothing would. And Lizzie could hardly wait to tell the vet that she had figured out Teddy's future. She was so proud of the little pup. She was positive he would be an excellent hearing dog.

The only thing was, she wasn't sure what to do next. She had thought about calling one of the centers she had found on the Internet, the ones that trained assistance dogs for deaf or disabled people. Most of them made it clear that they welcomed dogs from shelters and other rescue organizations, and that dogs of all shapes and sizes were trainable. Lizzie had loved looking at their websites, where she saw videos of the dogs in action, helping their human companions. It made her cry to see the beautiful bond between the people and their dogs, and to see how the dogs made such a difference in people's lives.

But Lizzie had decided to wait and talk to Dr. Gibson. The vet would probably know exactly who to call. "She'll figure it out," she whispered to Teddy now as she sat in the passenger seat of the van. Dr. Gibson had asked Lizzie to meet her at her office, where she was finishing up some paperwork before another busy week began.

"I hope you won't be too disappointed if this doesn't work out," her mother said as they pulled up at the vet's office. "Remember, Dr. Gibson was looking for a home for Teddy. She may have something else in mind for him." She reached over to pet Teddy. "In any case, I'm sure she'll be impressed with what you've taught him. I sure am. You did a good job, Lizzie."

Lizzie ducked her head. "Thanks." She opened the car door. "So, remember, in five minutes you'll knock on the door, right?"

"Got it." Mom tousled Lizzie's hair.

Lizzie took a deep breath. "Okay, Teddy. Ready to show your stuff?"

Teddy glanced up at her with his shiny black eyes. His fluffy tail thumped against her chest and he let out a little woof.

Let's go! Let's do it!

Lizzie laughed and kissed his nose. "I agree. You *are* ready." She led him up to the vet's front door.

That first night after she'd talked to Maria, Lizzie had read all about hearing dogs. She'd learned that it usually took about six months of training for a dog to learn to be his human companion's ears. The dog learned to hear things that his deaf owner might miss. Like the sound of someone calling his owner's name. Or a teakettle whistling, or a doorbell, or the ringing of the phone. Or a baby's cry. A dog was ready to work when he could identify at least three sounds, alert his owner, and lead her to the sound.

Teddy wasn't quite there yet, but Lizzie had made a start. She was sure Teddy could learn much, much more. All she had to do now was convince Dr. Gibson. She crossed her fingers and knocked on the door.

"Hello, Lizzie. Hello, Teddy." Dr. Gibson opened the door with a smile.

As Lizzie led him into the empty waiting room,

Teddy began to spin and bark. Lizzie clapped her hands, three loud, sharp claps. Teddy paused for a second to look at her. "Good boy," she said. "Down."

Teddy dropped to the floor, still looking up at Lizzie.

"Good boy," she said again. She tossed him a piece of hot dog. Teddy gobbled it up and sprang to his feet, but this time he did not spin and bark. He stood waiting, watching Lizzie carefully to find out what to do next.

"Wow," said Dr. Gibson. "That's very impressive."

Lizzie shrugged. "He already knew how to lie down on command," she said. "At least his first owners must have cared enough to take him to obedience classes. All I did was figure out that asking him to sit or lie down was a good way to stop him from barking and spinning around. If he's lying down, he can't spin. And if he can't spin, he doesn't get as excited, so he doesn't bark."

Dr. Gibson nodded. "That makes sense." She sat down in one of the waiting-room chairs, and Lizzie sat down next to her. "On the phone, you said that you had an idea for Teddy's future. I have a few ideas, too. What is yours?"

Lizzie gulped. Maybe this had all been for nothing, if Dr. Gibson had other plans for Teddy. She checked her watch. Her mom would be knocking on the door any minute. "I think he could be an assistance dog," she said. "A hearing dog, for someone who's deaf. Teddy notices everything. That's part of why he barks so much. But I think he could be trained to notice things for a purpose — to be someone's ears."

"Hmmm." Dr. Gibson raised her eyebrows. "Very interesting. But —"

Just then, there was a knock at the door. Teddy sprang to his feet and stared at the door. Then, instead of barking, he ran to Lizzie and put a paw up on her leg. "Is someone at the door?" Lizzie asked. He pawed at her again, until she stood up. Then he ran to the door, checking over his shoulder to see if she was following him.

Lizzie felt like her heart might burst from pride. She threw open the door and grinned at her mom. Teddy had pulled off the "trick" she'd taught him, acting exactly like the hearing dogs in the videos she'd seen. "He did it," she said, beaming.

"Yay for Teddy!" Mom yelled.

At that, Teddy began to bark and spin. This time, Lizzie just laughed and let him do his thing. He deserved it. She looked over at Dr. Gibson. "What do you think?" she asked. Her heart was beating fast.

"I think that's quite amazing," said the vet.

"He doesn't do it every time," Lizzie confessed. "Not nearly. But with some training . . ."

Dr. Gibson nodded slowly, looking very serious. "Lizzie," she said, "I can see that you've worked very hard with Teddy. I'd like you to keep him for one more night. But then there's someone I want him to meet."

CHAPTER TEN

"I still can't believe it," Lizzie said, as she and her Mom drove back to the vet's office the next afternoon. "After all that work I did with Teddy, Dr. Gibson is still going to take him away." She buried her nose in the little dog's ruff and breathed in his special puppy smell. She had become very, very attached to Teddy in the short time she'd had him. All the training they had done together had made her feel even more bonded to the cute pup.

Last night, after she had set her dog figurines back on the shelf and rehung her "Dog Breeds of the World" poster, Teddy had slept curled up in her arms. For one night, Lizzie had pretended that Teddy was hers, that dog of her very own. But she knew it wasn't true. She knew that if she wanted to keep fostering puppies, her family could not adopt another full-time dog. Teddy would have to find another owner, one who would love him as much as she did. She hoped Dr. Gibson had found someone who deserved this special dog. But who could it be? "I wonder where we're bringing him today," Lizzie said to her mom for the fifth time.

"Let's be patient and find out," said Mom. She pulled into the vet's parking lot. Dr. Gibson must have been watching for them, because she came right out and climbed into the van.

"Hi, everybody," she said. "This is exciting. I sure hope my friend Matthew likes Teddy." She told Mom which way to go.

"Who is Matthew?" asked Lizzie, as they headed down the street.

"Remember I told you about a friend of mine whose dog was very old and sick?" Dr. Gibson asked. "Well, that was Matthew. His dog died just a few days ago. Actually, it was on the same day I stopped by. The same day —"

"As the ambulance incident?" Mom asked.

Dr. Gibson gave a little cough. "That's right. I may have been a little hard on you that day, Lizzie — but it was partly because I was upset about Leo dying. He was the sweetest old black Lab, and Matthew loved him so."

Lizzie felt tears come to her eyes. It was always so sad to hear about a dog dying. "I'm sorry," she said. "I'm sorry for Matthew."

"That's not all," said Dr. Gibson. "Matthew is — or was — a soldier. He left the service about a year ago. He —" She cleared her throat again. "Matthew was wounded in action. He lost his hearing when something exploded very close to him. He's lucky to be alive, but his life has not been easy. Losing Leo is extra hard on him because of that."

"So — do you think Teddy could be his hearing dog?" Lizzie sat up in her seat, excited. "That would be so cool."

"Easy, Lizzie," said Dr. Gibson. "There are a lot of ifs here. That's why I didn't want to say anything last night. First of all, Teddy has to be evaluated by a trainer. I have a good friend at Hearing Buddies, a program that trains these dogs. I spoke to her today, and she's agreed to see Teddy as soon as possible. I'd like to take him to see her tomorrow. She's also agreed that if he and Matthew are a good match, Teddy can be assigned to him when he finishes his training. I had to pull a few strings for that."

"Do you think Teddy and Matthew will be a good match?" Lizzie held her breath, waiting for the answer.

"I have no idea," said Dr. Gibson. "Teddy is as different from Matt's last dog, Leo, as night is from day. I'm thinking that might be a good thing, since Matthew is still very sad about Leo. I'm hoping Teddy will make him laugh, distract him a little. Matthew is more of a big-dog kind of guy — but Teddy has a big-dog personality. So I'm hoping for the best."

"You never know," said Lizzie. "Remember Bandit? I never thought he'd end up with a big, tough guy — but he did, and it's working out great." Bandit was a fluffy little Shih Tzu the Petersons had fostered. Dr. Gibson knew him well, since he had needed some medical attention.

She laughed. "You're so right," she said. "So let's

cross our fingers and hope that Teddy charms Matthew."

A few minutes later, they pulled up at a small yellow house. "Here we are," said Dr. Gibson. "I'll go in first and make sure Matthew is ready for this. He knows I'm bringing some friends over, with a dog — but that's all he knows, so far."

Lizzie and Mom waited in the van with Teddy while Dr. Gibson went into the house. Lizzie petted Teddy's head and ears, trying to calm herself down. This was Teddy's big chance.

A few minutes later, Dr. Gibson waved from the front porch. "Come on in," she called.

Lizzie, Mom, and Teddy walked up to the door. Lizzie's heart was pounding. "Be a good boy, Teddy," she said.

Once they were inside, Dr. Gibson introduced Lizzie and her mom to Matthew. He was very tall and very handsome, and Lizzie felt herself blushing as she shook his hand.

"Matthew is great at lipreading," said Dr. Gibson. "Just make sure you are facing him and speak slowly and clearly."

"Hi, Matthew." Lizzie looked straight into his serious face. "I'm really sorry about your dog, Leo."

Matthew nodded. His eyes were full of sadness. "Thank you," he said in a thick voice. "I miss him." He looked down at the small orange pup. "And this must be Teddy."

Hearing his name, Teddy barked and began to spin excitedly.

Quickly, Lizzie clapped her hands. "Quiet, Teddy," she said. "Lie down."

Obediently, Teddy dropped to the floor.

Matthew raised an eyebrow. "He listens to you," he said. "Very good." He knelt down to pet Teddy's soft fur, and Teddy rolled over to show his pink puppy belly.

Lizzie crossed her fingers, watching. She smiled when Matthew took Teddy into his arms and stood up with the tiny dog cradled in his big hands. Matthew's face was still serious as he held Teddy up so he could look into his eyes. "You are a tiny thing, aren't you?" he said.

Dr. Gibson caught Lizzie's eye and pointed toward the door. The vet raised her eyebrows. Then she slipped outside and closed the door behind her.

Lizzie tugged on Matthew's sleeve. "Want to see what he can do?" she asked when he looked at her.

Matthew nodded and put Teddy down.

A moment later, Dr. Gibson knocked at the door. At the sound, Teddy spun around once and let out three sharp barks. Lizzie watched Matthew's expression. She could tell that he couldn't hear a thing. Then Teddy did something wonderful. He took a few steps toward Matthew and put a paw on the tall man's pant leg.

Something's going on. Something you need to know about. Follow me!

Then the little dog turned and headed for the door, checking to see if Matthew was following him. Matthew gave Lizzie a questioning look. Then he followed Teddy to the door and opened it wide. "Well, hello! Look who's here." He opened the door wider for Dr. Gibson, then bent down to pet Teddy. "What a good boy," he said. "Aren't you smart!" He scooped the little dog up again and nuzzled his cheek against Teddy's.

"Matthew," said Dr. Gibson. "We think Teddy

could learn to be a hearing dog. I know it's too soon after Leo for you to think about another dog, but it would take at least six months to train Teddy. Maybe by then you'd be ready. What do you think?"

Matthew considered this. Then he bent his head to Teddy's again. "I think I could use a friend," Lizzie heard him murmur. "What do you say, little guy?"

A little while later, as she and her mom were on their way home, Lizzie blew her nose and wiped her eyes. Every time she thought of the look on Matthew's face she began to cry all over again. But this time, her tears were happy ones. Mostly, anyway. They had left Teddy with Matthew and Dr. Gibson. Tomorrow, Dr. Gibson would take the perky pup to meet her friend at the Hearing

Buddies center. Lizzie had hugged Teddy close; it wasn't easy to say good-bye to the little lovebug. But she'd known it was the right thing to do. She'd known for sure, as soon as she had seen the way Matthew's serious face changed when Teddy licked his cheek. "That was the first time I saw Matthew smile," she told her mom. "I think everything is going to work out perfectly, don't you?"

Mom glanced over at her. "I do," she said. "Thanks to you, I think Teddy has found the perfect home. And I think Matthew has found a friend. I'm really proud of you, sweetie." She put on her blinker and pulled into the shopping center. "How about if we celebrate with pizza and a movie?" she asked. "You can pick out a DVD at the video store while I order the food." She smiled at Lizzie and reached out to stroke her hair. "Let me guess. *101 Dalmatians*? *Marmaduke*? *Cats and Dogs*?"

Lizzie shook her head. "Maybe this time I'll get a movie about ice-skating, or a talking fish, or princesses." She grinned. "After all, everybody needs some balance in their lives — even me!"

PUPPY TIPS

A barking dog can be a real problem, for his owners and for neighbors. It's not always an easy problem to solve, either. Lizzie had the right idea with Teddy: She read all she could and tried to learn some different ways to solve the problem. Then she spent a lot of time working with him, without using harsh techniques like hitting or yelling.

If she needed more help or ideas, she could have also talked more with her veterinarian, Dr. Gibson, or with an animal behaviorist.

It can take a lot of time and patience to train a dog, but the results can be very worthwhile.

Dear Reader,

One of my favorite parts of my job as a writer is doing research and learning new things. Before I wrote this book I did not know very much about how dogs can help people who do not hear well. I did a lot of research, mostly on the Internet, and I learned a lot. Like Lizzie, I was very moved when I watched videos of service dogs working with their owners.

Yours from the Puppy Place,
Ellen Miles

P.S. To meet another puppy who needed an emergency foster home, read BELLA.

THE PUPPY PLACE

DON'T MISS THE NEXT PUPPY PLACE ADVENTURE!

Here's a peek at MOCHA!

"Hey, look at *that* place," Charles said, trying to change the subject. The weak winter sun had nearly set and long shadows crept along the snow-covered ground, but he could just make out a tall iron gate flanked by giant stone pillars. Beyond it, a driveway marked by tall trees on either side wound up the hill and disappeared into a forest of pine trees. "Imagine how gigantic that house must be, if that's just the gate."

"I'll bet your aunt and uncle aren't too thrilled about the way their town is changing," Mom said. "After all, they moved out of the city so they could have a simpler life." She turned the van up a long, bumpy unpaved driveway. "Here we are," she said. "At least their place hasn't changed at all."

Charles's aunt, uncle, and cousins came out onto the porch when the van pulled up. "Hello! It's so great to see you all," said Aunt Abigail. Amid a lot of hugs and "look how you've grown's," everyone helped unload the van. Soon all their stuff was piled in the front hallway: extra pots and pans for cooking the big dinner, suitcases, Charles's special favorite pillow, Mom's knitting stuff, Lizzie's sleeping bag, the Bean's toy fire truck, Buddy's bed and food dishes, Dad's hiking boots.

"We can only stay a few weeks," Mom joked, looking around at the huge pile.

"You're welcome as long as you want to be here," said Aunt Abigail. "You're my favorite sister-in-law, remember? And I'm so glad you were able to come a few days early. Stephen doesn't believe the weatherman, but if this ice storm they're predicting does show up, nobody will be going anywhere later this week."

Charles shifted from foot to foot as he half-listened to the grown-ups talking. Delicious cooking smells drifted in from the kitchen, and Charles's stomach grumbled. How long would it be until supper? He caught Becky's eye and made a funny face.

She started to laugh, but her giggles were drowned out by a loud knocking at the door.

Aunt Abigail raised her eyebrows. "Who could that be?" she said as she opened the door. There, in the shadows just beyond the yellow glow of the hall light, stood a tall dark man in a black suit.

"Hello," he said. "I'm hoping you can help me out."

When the man took a step forward into the light, Charles gasped.

The stranger on the doorstep had a puppy in his arms.

ABOUT THE AUTHOR

Ellen Miles loves dogs, which is why she has a great time writing the Puppy Place books. And guess what? She loves cats, too! (In fact, her very first pet was a beautiful tortoiseshell cat named Jenny.) That's why she came up with a brand-new series called Kitty Corner. Ellen lives in Vermont and loves to be outdoors every day, walking, biking, skiing, or swimming, depending on the season. She also loves to read, cook, explore her beautiful state, play with dogs, and hang out with friends and family.

Visit Ellen at www.ellenmiles.net.